Fuck
The Bitch in the
Mouth

Discriminating & Incriminating Poetry
By An
Intimidating Poet
Who Doesn't Give A Shit About Anything
Save His Gigantically Delicious Cock

Walter Joseph Schenck, Jr.

Written on a dare.
Published in the belief of the
First Amendment Right
to write-and have published whatever the fuck
I want to write and publish.

Contents

Internet Porno Feast Failure

Fuck the bitch in the mouth
Flip her over, like a pancake
Fuck the cunt in the ass.
Toss her aside.
Fuck the queer in the mouth,
Flip him over, like toast,
Fuck the queer in the ass
Then together upload the triathlon thrill
      to the Internet
In hopes of a zillion hotti-hot hits.
Makes some bucks for the cunts exhibiting
      pristine joy –
But truthfully, the Internet is chuck full of
Bitches fucking doggies and horses
And queers on queers
And cunts on cunts,
      so who will want to view
Another boring performance of
      three soul mates
Intercoursing rectums and mouths.
Like the houting fish,
extinction becomes the
Erection's sad demise,
Maybe like a Thomas Jefferson statue
Who knew how to build a secret room
In his mansion for his personal jenny gal.

Update: Father Priest in New Orleans must have read this poem,
he and his two cunts a-fucking on the altar, camera ready.

Truthfully, I ravish the kill,
The decapitation, the shattering,
The torching of bronze heads
    and marble insults;
For the icons:
    political and religious,
        have no righteous right to exist
An insult against the deep-set morality
    of a moralist
Hating supremacy in all fashions.

Add this truthful reality to this poem
    God, the righteous one that is,
        Not the fairy tale one,
Hates statues, without exception,
    demanding their destruction,
So for Trumpy baby to write an
    executive order forbidding decimation
Puts him squarely against God.

I didn't say this. No, not I,
But Jeremiah talked the
    point of law concerning
        statue status to Josiah
before Josiah met his Necho in Megiddo.

Blackface Nigger

I'm a blackface nigger . . .
    Oh, oh, oh
I'm a blackface nigger . . .
    Oh, oh, oh.

Tap dancing on the stage next to
    Shirley Temple
Cutsy girl no protest, but adorable
Tip top hat and pearl handle cane
    Oh, ah, oh, ah.

Tap dancing blackface nigger,
Why ain't there no black men dancing
    the tap . . .
        Singing the song . . .
            wearing the tip top hat . . .

Why ain't you doing the reverse?
Wearing white face to depict the honkey
    Roaring your
        war paint on the streets
Carrying your lasso, singing
    African Doodle Dandy?

I confess, I can't remember . . .
    did George M. Cohan
        wear black face
Tap dancing underneath
    the spotlight of gory?

Or, should I say,
    the bathing revelation of shame?

    Can't stop:
Did Custer say to Sitting Bull,
"Indian, don't wear-um red paint on cheek. Me got-ta-me six
shooters to

Shot-a-your-ass dead,
          dead,
                    dead.

Joke's on Custer, Sitting Bull aim-um
Good arrow-shot, long blond hair,
A gone . . . gone . . . gone

Many white boys to follow.

Oh Fuck, update: Netflick's move, Cuties,
just made me a boring bore with nothing to bore away at.
Frechie's always gotta go where no one else will: Netflick
endorsed, ratified, and ready to become a 10-year series.

A Nigger can murder a Nigger
But never can a cracker trash kill a cracker

    One-year old baby killed
No riots there.

    Anyone want-a visit St. Louis
Where private streets and security gates
Don't mean a fucking thing?
Hey, white boys
(Because that's all I could see doing the rioting),
Why haven't you gone to pe/lu/shit's house?
    Oh, I know the answer.
Envy-filled impoverished rioter left his tap dancing shoes at
home.
    Can't wait for the prosecutor to lose
her case, so St. Louis
privileged and private citizens
can hire mercenaries armed with M-60's
to kill and main all trespassers
with immunity-impunity!
My castle is my castle
and you just ain't welcomed.
Celebrate!
Decapitated heads and amputated arms
are a-rolling down the street!

Therefore, stupid-ass trespassers,
When a gate has the word
"Private Street" written in bold letters,
Don't enter, because shooting time is
Legal and who gives a fuck about a
cracker's corpse, cause like
a nigger killing a nigger,
it's all in the right frame of social acceptance and the violators'
name will instantly be forgotten.

Where in the hell is Ferguson?

I witnessed on Silver Street
In Jacksonville, Fl an attempted rally,
White boys holding BLM signs
Before the noonday's sun could burn their
    tender white skins black.

Not knowing what to do,
    idling and milling about
They looked for a chanter to lead
Not one to be found
Then approached a black man
    who slid on by
Confused why so many white boys held
    so many BLM signs.

Not knowing what to do in his
    status of honorarium
He struck his fist into the air
    for the briefest second
Then high-tailed the hell away from whitey
Before whitey-mighty realized a black man
Invaded their precious protest
            That black lives matter.

Part 2

Came across in front of CVS
    on Race Tack Road
The same scenario,
Privilege white boys,
economically far above Silver Street's
    placard holders
        seeking a chanter to lead
          till someone lead the rant
confusing the fuck out of
    kiddie accomplice
who probably never met a black person
    ever never, but maybe so, who knows,
being Hispanic
I ain't a member of their society
living in their exclusive white-ass
    filled neighborhood.
If there are black families around,
    don't forget white bastards
        to pay not only homage
as you hold your placards
    but reparations as well . . .
$350,000 to each, while
    forgetting reparation to the white trash
Irish who died on the battlefield,
    but so-what that an Irish lad
sacrificed his life for a cause
    that impoverished his son, needing a
Vietnam to hone his protesting skills,
not one water cannon fired
    at white boy's rioting feast.

Once I heard,
    I think I did,
        Maybe I imagined it . . .

    "If I were in Birmingham, I would have thrown myself in
front of the water cannon, a smile on my face who's seared skin
enflamed throughout America, love."

I imagined it.
    No white boy ever seared his skin
        In Birmingham.

But wow!
Whitey loves to tear down statues,
Their protest after getting an "F'
In history class, the subject way too
    Painful and sensitive
        for their social growth.

It's okay. God says
In front of the naked cheerleader,
"Go Boy, Go!'
    Tear them down,
        Make me a Happy God!"

The water cannons are shut off.

Biden's Basement

With a TV, a beer, a camera,
Who needs to campaign on the streets?
Let the poor cocksucker do it.
Corona-19, the
campaign workers to catch.
Not that inflammatory disease
for Biden who waits to sit on the throne
for Obama to dangle Biden's strings
for invisible Biden, dead on arrival,
his corpse stinky like a useless wiley,
but who cares, if he can't get up
for his old poster picture suffices for
the mindless Demon-rats
who on day one destroyed America
in its surrender to little rocket man.
I better pull out all my money from the bank, employ me some whores,
Pimping them for demon-rats' consumption.
Poor corpse of a replacement press-corps
unable to phantom the reason why the young Girlie is on her
knees, her tongue ready to swallow an ejaculation never to cum.

Update: Damn, can't finish a poem before it becomes obsolete:
Pelosi's gonna get rid of Biden based on a 25th Amendment
additive, old boy gonna have to go to pasture with the cows
mumbling who knows what as he steps into the cow's shit, as if
he shit ain't already high enough.

90-day poem, then so what,
Cowardly Biden

Hey, can't meet Chris Wallace – he's too smart. The candidate is not handsome, not young, not mentally acute, but acute cutie's point broke off, the basement dweller can't answer the questions, ain't gonna try – so me and my tv and popcorn are going have to be enough to rouse my intrigue if VP can talk – not a vip, but indeed a viper, heard, time will tell, if debate enacted to enact a remedy, or like a plagiarized TV commercial, taking credit where done deserved, suddenly Biden's name is changed from a noun to a verb, like a Bork.

Hey, is this statement miserable fakery, or something perhaps on the cusp of a cuspy thing-a-gig. I got me a hundred-million followers who care not if I live in a basement. All we need is a tv, popcorn, hotdogs, and beer. I know I'm-a-going-to win because we basement dwellers all gotta stick together – me and my obedient slaves.

Education ain't needed in the ghetto – just guns, heroine, prostitutes, so big-boy white politician can maintain his million-dollar mansion, a-smiling, a-smiling, a-smiling.
Oh, it's so good to be popular. Who needs brains? Not this vip of a viper.

Think I'm wrong? Ask Cal Cunningham, candidate for North Carolina's senate seat – YES – a fucking Democrat – sorry, a demon-rat, who just can't wait to pull off a Clinton act – and why is it the North Carolinians prefer an immoralist over a moralist, unless the whole state is texting for desired pussy conquest? If so, go on with your orgy. But don't pray for forgiveness, as this poem, equal to Jeremiah's outcry, has condemned you, regardless of your pleads. Too late, soul-destroyers.

10

Though they
hide, hide, hide,
In November
they
thrive, thrive, thrive
unlike brood IX's cicadas
chirping chirps
(That's a 9 in case you're too stupid to figure out the IX)
an outpouring noise
for sexual consumption
imitated perfectly by the Demon-rats of Seattle, Baltimore,
Oakland
—and boy-oh-boy—
Rioting paradise Portland – that is POX
(like a plague that pocks throu' the streets of flames)
who needs a consumptive power
to cleanse their stupidity
before they breed into the world
haters demanding an empty revolution
like Attila the German boy
left Fredo Rome vacant.

For the ignorant:
Fredo is a dumb ass loser
A rapacious identification for Demon-rats.

Don't believe me?
Ask pe/louse/shit the traitor
and,
Cuomo who ain't on TV anymore.

Poor White Trash Bitch

At the university I met a white trash bitch
Who said, "I'll do anything for you."
Taking her at her word I replied,
"Take off your pants,"
And before I could flutter my eyelids
came off everything
her mouth wide open,
so I fucked the bitch in the mouth
who fell in love with my gigantic cock
who failed in all her subjects
not giving a shit about anything but her
day long / night long obsession with my
gigantic cock in her mouth
using it as if a thumb throughout the night,
I, never having to wash Mr. Penis for her
Mouth not only cleansed
my cherished cock cleaner
Than my armpits, but the bitch's mouth
became the receptor for my shit as well.

That cunt of cunts I finally left, replacing her
With three others who strived with all their hearts to bathe my
soul clean with their
          flickering tongues,
those four the first of 2,996
to show up somehow at my doorstep, at work, in the theater, in
the streets,
the reputation of my cock a firm guarantee of
excellent pleasure always to cum.

This is page 13.
If you're still reading my deplorable protests
Than you must be a thriller-filler-diller-liver
Or a regressive nut case bored to hell with
All the pure shit nonsense of other poets who
Write of love and the bees or write deep
virtuous messages needing an analysis,
But not so with me for I get to the point.
Somewhere within these filthy pages,
Coated with glee, evident undeniable
I'm a cussing man
Bathed in the mire of offensive pleasures.
Thus and so, who gives a damn about a comma or misspelled
word,
for in shit-embraced wordage
there are no rules
exactly as the protestors demand their reading
material to reflect sacred values of something
sacred, but I just don't know what that sacred
value is unless it's to dig up Mao and Lenin,
grinding their maggot filled consumed ugliness into a chow soup
delight, delicious.
No Shelley or Wordsworth for me
Though 50 years ago I done-did master them
As a masturbator's fantasy come true.
Hey, 50 years from now,
Me and my filth will become classical
Mandatory reading for grade school rebels.
Shakespeare taught me super well.

Me? A racist?

Depends on ignoramus, not my mouth.
My writing says I'm a racist, yet I fucked
More black girlfriends than white,
So yeah, white pussy I don't like
As much as black pussy, so I am a racist,
So when I have a party with 20 black girls
And one white girl . . .
the evidence is in the bedroom
that black pussy has no equal.

Well, goodness gracious
Why did it take so long to figure out the
      obvious?
Didn't I write it plainly enough
      twenty-five years ago?
Oh, sorry, no one reads anything I write,
All those prophetic poems dusting away
While the world wonders why it's in trouble.
All the leaders need do is read
what I announced during my premium
state when my premium mind exposed an
unprecedented quality of exposed material.
But to read a derogatory condemnation
Takes a perverted mind,
Political correctness be damned to hell,
so like the time when Jeremiah's
scrolls got burned by Jehoiakim
And Jerusalem's wall breached, so shall the world be breached,
the spectators of a fearful
Hour's event shuddering while a copy of my
book burns in the bookstore
of
      dismal
                  disregard.
By the way, what religious maniac is not
Comparable to a criminal? For example,
      what non-denominational freak is
      different from the controlling
      lynchpins of Iran? Had the Shia been a
Christian, all his subjects would now be
Adored by the media fakers,
      ratified by the world,
As truth seekers on a journey of deep
Immersive exploration into the soul's
Essence with God. Hey, look at the Buddhists
Who mastered the art of deception,
Christian media broadcasting their shit-scum

Lies as though immaculate revelations. You Iranians just don't
get it, do you?
Smile when you look down the barrel of a
Six-shooter, and the world will smile with you.

Afterall, isn't the world immune to Indians shitting on the street
and throwing their candy wrappers on the sidewalk?

Hey! Hey! Where does the ashes of a fried Indian corpse end up?
Down the river? Inside a fish's stomach? Or, on the dinner table
after everything mingled with everything else?

Wow! Reincarnation's gotta be a genuine being:
          therefore be.

I once wanted to be an American,
>   But now I want to be an Inca.
1,000-year-old building still standing
>   Compared to a fifth span of time
For Grecian imitation architecture
Dots the strife-torn landscape of U.S.A.,
While Inca majesty boldly touches the clouds of lavender
sunsets, tourist demanding a
Visitation, permitted because they will go away, unlike the
crazed illegals, who want to
Stay in an unwelcoming culture of racist extremists. The Inca
knows full well the Spaniards' hatred, their cannons and
enslavement a thing embraced by the crackers
Who dare to announce themselves freeman
While chaining and subverting all darkies to
suffer indignity in a land of lies where equality
is only for white-ass motherfuckers,
and this is no lie,
White boys indeed fuck their mothers. Just
ask any Greek playwright who teaches Greek
Philosophy while building on their campuses in every city,
Greek architecture.
The perverted queers just never go away
Loving to fuck mama's ass.

Fucking sons of bitches, asshole manipulators
Are at it again, cheating, stealing, manipulating
The liars akin to thieves, self-serving.

GET OUT OF THE UN
The fuckers ain't united except to fake
     USA out of its money.
Same with Germany – GET OUT!

The senators who voted to stop American
Forces from leaving South Korea . . .
Fuck you son-of-bitches, you know nothing
     about shit-eating North Korea,
          unless its bribes you took?
Who knows the compulsion that compelled
     You miserable senators
               – with a small "s"
To force our military to remain in a country
where five minutes after the button is pushed
No more alive those American soldier boys.

What? They're there to discourage an
     invasion? You fucking idiots!
That crazy fat boy doesn't give a damn!
China-punk's navy is on fat boy's side,
So forget about being South Korea's savior,
And turn to Taiwan to save them before
China boats land on their shores right
After they landed on Hong Kong's shores.
No more Samsung for thee,
Foolish senator scum-bag.
Don't believe me? Ask Jimmy Lai.
But don't ask Navid Afkari because the Iranians done did hung
him,
Hoping to quell the audience, but
They forgot to turn off the Internet;
so mouth, though murdered, speaks louder than ever.

Rep. Ted Yoho, bless his heart,
May have said what others think,
Perhaps intentionally, or not, or may never have said on the
Capital steps of D.C.,
a "fucking bitch," to she so she can prove otherwise, but never
did, anyhow, a fact is a fact.

If hungry, break a window, kill the wealthy,
After taxing them for everything they have.

Jobless New York city,
A tribute to she who must be Pelooshit's
Favorite rep in the U.S.A.

Where were the cellphones cameras?

Oh, hey, fucking update: No Amazon in Brooklyn, so taxes gotta
go higher to make up for the job losses.

Yep, you guys voted for her. Real smart.

Now it is supposed she wants another job promotion to Senator.
Serves you right, because you're the ones who gave out the inch.

Tried to hop on a bus in downtown, midtown, going uptown, but
ain't got me a mask. Bus driver, captain of health, told me get
out, and that's okay, cause I got me a weapon in my pocket.
Breaking his nose ain't enough, gotta go for his ribs, for his
fingers, until the fuckin' bus driver, captain of health, knows he
ain't the fucking boss of my coronavirus, for it's the mandate
announced for Corona-to-survive that he's messing with.

Hey, motherfucker, same thing with bouncers at the bar, I ain't
need of a mask,
I got me a 38 caliber in my glove compartment of my hotrod dud
of a car, and come out a-shooting I will, caring nothing who I
hurt, for Mr. Coronavirus gotta survive.

Hey, me and my pal intent to get rid of
cronies who tell me no mask, no entry, so
fuck you all, I got a baseball bat, a 38 cal.,
and nerves of steel to shoot em anyone who
dares interfere with my freedom to spread
throughout the world Mr. Coronavirus
mandate to survive.

This ain't all folks:

Mr. Corona-virus killer wants-a go-killing
Airline passengers and captains,
Don't forget the stewardess, in 3D no doubt,

Now on August 5th, bang, wham!
Australia's really brought out the hatred, no punches barred,
against the protectors of society, sovereign rights too important,
so main and destroy the female cop
By smashing her skull into the concrete sidewall, she who dared
to ask for a violator to help protect society by covering her face,
but no, Mr. Corona-virus, (now I know

He's got a twelve-inch cock) whispered to the unmasked
attacker: kill, kill, kill, make the news, 5 minute-fame yours just
for giving me a few more victims, enflaming their innards with
rabid mutation.

Mmmmm, how I love stupid, self-centered
Bastards and bitches. One billion dead my goal. Thank you,
protestors and enforcers of no-mask rights, for your cooperation.

She thinks she knows how to stimulate a nickname everlasting, saggy tits and wrinkled shit, but when I think of her degenerate affiliation with slavery's top endorser, the Democrat Party, I know I wanna throw her ice cream in her face while she secretly pleads with Carson not to build black housing units among the houses of her walled-in paradise, a liberal dreamers concept of granting residential equality to 100% black residents that she can't abide by, pretending all the time to love black souls while her white soul is in agony over the fact she ain't got a slave in her basement, or two, to clean her house.

Therefore, her hushed mouth ignores the demise of the Affirmatively Furthering Fair Housing Rule, (AFFH) Obama's sneak attack on suburbia dreamed up by unelected fraudsters to mighty dignity, much to her relief.

I think now we should allow underpaid Hispanics to move into her housing area. I also think the FBI should plan a pre-dawn raid on her house with FOX News outside and sharp shooters running amuck, akin to Stone the man, who thankfully has a true friend in the best part of the neighborhood.

Yep, went to school with the measles,
me and my buddy,
who never got a polio shot,
two classmates with read blisters
spreading it to all,
two heroes,
for everyone wanted to escape from the
    stifling classroom,
but that polio got only him,
not the rest of us,
he becoming a bigger hero than us
    red-pimpled idiots
for he went on to care about humanity
while the rest of us
went on toward personal vendettas,
brought on by the pimpled terror
with only shingles waiting for us old folk
too damn worn out and useless to give a fuck
except that you all better not fuck with our Medicare or S.S.
check.
Don't forget young punk ass
We oldies fought all the wars . . . victoriously.

White Spectacle

An inspiring truth discovered in an article
On FOX News, morning of July 27, 2020
So true, black equality rights again fucked
By a crazed rally of white boys
—cracker heads—
Subversive penis lovers who dreamt
Of mama's pussy gone unfulfilled,
So to the streets they go-a-burning
Hurting papa-figure policeman
With Molotov cocktails, rocks, and fire
Trying to burn away history for it suits them
        Not, their idea society not even
                Fathomed, for they know not what to
                    Aspire to, so busy masturbating
All anarchists wanting a camera on the
        cuming moment.
Meantime, what white citizen does not look upon a black
innocent who merely wants
To shop without stares of hate that
        Yesterday was not there?
Factually, Antifa-da-mother bitch,
Has a truckload of chains and whips, not to
Overthrow white men's rule, but to
        Institute their own rule: they the
                Masterclass, a thousand deceptive
                    Hitlers, a-hitting their way to
                        power.
Take the pledge, foolish people.
I read Oedipus Rex seven times!
Then, published it!

"Intensified Peace"

Oakland, California protestors,
set fire to the courthouse,
Aimed fireworks at cops
Burned down the police station,
Why stop there?
Living legacy has yet to encompass
        the burning of the capital.
So go on in your quest to burn.
Don't forget the forest and the water works
Facilities, so when the firehouse's water done-gone dry, no water
ever again to put out the fire between your breeches.

Make sure you don't run out of hotdogs
        During the feast time of a country
                Set ablaze with no agenda
                        Established except to give the
                                Arsonists a merry good time.

Actually, so sorry, peacefully filled
Exhilaration.

Oh, look, your own house and car's on fire
while you're sleeping, your face caught on video, the vengeful
business owners and cops knowing where you live.

Boo, hoo.

Especially Obama, the white boy
who yearns to be black, and the blacks,
desiring a blackie, readily accepts him as a blackie. I blame the
white boys for that, their prejudice kicking him out from the
white world. Thus, I wonder if Levin ain't right,
Obama's a pathological liar, some sort of psychosis there, but
what do I know? Nothing at all. I'm a stupid ass, but at least I
can testify I'm an ignorant cocksucker. I don't know if whitey-
blackie is a liar, as I don't know either one of them, but the news
article caught my eye and inspired me to write this, but as to
taking sides, well, the half-and-half is a demonrat and Levin's a
Reppie dude, so the Reppie dude wins.

So, why is Hannity afraid, his heart five times in fear while mine
is ten times cheering for Trumpy baby. Didn't Levin just
announce we have in our mist a Demon-rat pathological liar? –
Sorry, make that plural.

Gotta now mention another half-white wanting to be all-white –
that Cali girl, her name not worth a damn, who married a white
boy so three-quarter white her children, yeah, she represents
100% blacks, no ghetto girl there, white privilege upbringing.
Ha. Ha. You believe that shit?

Fuck Face	= A Democrat
Nigger hater	= A Democrat
Jim Crow laws	= A Democrat
A Cocksucker	= A Democrat
Shit-eating slimeball	= A Democrat
Slave enactor	= A Democrat
Civil War Perpetrator	= A Democrat
Socialism	= A Democrat
Leftist Hypocrite	= A Democrat
Mail-In Ballot Fraud	= A Democrat
Impeachment liars	= A Democrat
Benghazi	= A Democrat

My, my, alas, woe is me!

Pain, agony, suffering,

A Democrat's happiness!

Attackee Chineenaman

Neat-o, attackee chineenaman
His consularloosa-fill-a-max
Spy-boy equiptment.
But, didn't I tell you lazy-ass ameericannos?
Warned you of Costa Rican stadium jukee-mass equipto-filled
saucer up in the mountains, good catching-them cosmic rays
Of info galore, El Savador too, so say I, but who cares, Houston
so late in the game,
When next that Loss-of-angeeloose-a in
Cali-adnormal-state of madness gone awry.
Howeeveer-o I admit, LA a good hiding place for la-chino boy
who a-spies to spillo that jello so easy to obtain.
What intellectual property can possibly stem from a bunch of
stupid ass ameericos?

I don't know it Disease

I tell you man, we gotta be ready for the next disease.

What is the next disease?

I don't know?

Is it going to come from a bacteria? A flea? A rat? A dog? A cat? A deer tick? A mosquito? A Bat?

Man, I don't know, but we gotta be ready?

How do we prepare?

I don't know. We gotta invest billions.

On what?

I don't know. But it's critical to be ready.

Shall we quarantine?

Yes, yes. Yes.

Who? Us? Them?

I don't know. But we gotta be ready. Spend on a whim a trillion. We gotta be ready.

Shall we quarantine Africa? Costa Rica? Brazil?

All of them?

China also?

No, no, they're the problem solvers. Give them a trillion?

For what?

To resolve the inevitable.

Which is?

The disease, man, why don't you understand. The humanity killing disease! It's our demise man.

Need then we go to China?

Who else got the nerve to save us? America done gone away to the lowest denominator.

So China's got the answer?

Fuck you, man, they are the answer. If they ain't, they'll give us the problem, so we gotta be ready. Don't you understand? We gotta load up the bomb and send it ASAP to Chineeman: bombs away, why don't you understand?

This evening's news: What was once the world is no more, seven billion souls rotting in the streets following the rally cry: We gotta be ready.

Treacherous night. We weren't ready.

Hey, lookey here I say, I acquired for me a list of abusive names for women:

Cunt, tramp, whore, bitch, semen eater, I can buy ten of you for a dime.

Yet to be fair, I also acquired for me a list as well for man tramps:

Degenerate, Scum-bag, Douche bag, Retart, Dirt bag, Cocksucker, Queer, Fuckhead, Asshole, Jackoff, Stupid Ass.

Unlike the women, the male words begin with a capital letter.

Now, let's add "Bork" to the list.

Neat-O this abusive collection for the writer in need of a derogatory word, or two, or three. But if you cuss and rage like me then you truly need to convert mereism to shankism.

Hey, how can we take the word "███" and place it in the dictionary as a word meaning shamed degenerate scam-blame?

How can we reinvent a noun to an active verb? Is it possible to make the word "███" to represent all the filthy, nasty, and degrading words to make all other bad words seem sweet? Shall I begin by asking a nun or a Catholic hospital? Will someone there say there is an ultimate betrayer of innocents who want to reside in a pure status without political corruption? Will they say their peace of mind has been permanently upset by learning they must, by legislative dictate enable abortions at their own expense? I mean, aren't Catholics supposed to be against abortions?

But, what the fuck do I know?

It may be possible that on October 22, 2020 twelve Catholic Democrat Senators will think it's okay to kill babies and sell their baby parts by their refusal to vote for confirmation of an originalist thinker.

We need to wait and see if time will create an exclamation point, an authenticity for a verb to come to end all verbs.

Meantime, rack up the baby parts, Catholic Democrat Senators, for if you vote against determined she then you will certainly endorse the abortion of babies, creating a verb of singular hostility. This new cuss word, ██████, a deceitful verb, legislative wise, representing hypocritical Democrat Catholic Senators.

"Hey, he's a ██████."

(Sorry - new cuss word blocked out by
Twitter and Facebook!
I guess I have been "Hunterized!")

Goddamn Chicken Wings

Those goddamn chicken wings from Brazil the real culprit taking
flight throughout chineerman's country,
Brazil guilty as hell, Ecuador too,
for fishing the bad shrimp,
so better sent 'em ships to Galapagos Islands
justified in stealing big fishees
for chineerman's plate.

By the power of we eat'em
The world must bow down to China
So chineerman can get fat
off the lay of the land –
Oh,
the ocean's as well.

Fuken' Garden

I understand perfectly why
Adam got so damned pissed off at God.
Plant a plant, it grows, then dies. The
miserable well-laid out plan gone awry
with all those dead bushes, and insects
stinging the head and arms and legs,
wanna make me damn God as well, such a
task should have been given to banana
eating monkeys, but nope,
mankind gotta suffer a planting.

No wonder Cain wanted a city and slaves.
Me too. A city and slaves.
All I need is a big stick, a sharp-edged rock,
and away I go,
a-slaving and a-killing
so my godman fucken' garden
can prosper with me never getting stung
again by a yellow jacket, bee, or a mosquito.

Wow, my fingernails,
   for once,
      are actually clean.

Ne'er knew my hands could get so smooth
For doing nothing more than whamming
My big stick on top of someone's head.

Stupidity manifests itself clearly in the
UN Security Council, (what security?)
this 15th day of August, 2020,
Iran with jets and bombs and
shot-em-up rifles and missiles
attack choppers at/tack/ing
so why the fuck is the U. S. of A. still in
the UN? Pull out, man the war ships, load the bombs, away we
go, Tehran no more.
If Beijing also, then let it be also.
JCPoA – for those who can't deciper –
Joint Comprehensive Plan of Action,
Is now incomprehension and unjointed, and certainly lacking
action, therefore unneeded,
The mighty men of Iran laughing and spitting at the U.S. of A. as
they invade for real, Syria, forget Iraq,
already Iran's puppet,
The hung man riotously happy for the
Muck-of-a-mess, for only so long can the chicken shout the sky
is falling – for with
an arms embargo who can sell bullets?
Better to murder a hundred million than to let the manufacturing
plants sit empty.

Can't wait for the biblical sword to be
made a plowshare.

Biben a fuck-up?
Don't know. Ask Obama.

Not my words – Obama's reputed words, don't know, no tape
recorder to verify,
But possibly true; waiting for a refute . . .
If a refute's possible. Time will tell if
Obama said it or not, but who cares –
For I doubt it not others have said it
During decades past – but since I'm not an
insider to things spoken, I can do nothing
more than speculate, wondering if my wondering
is correct or if
Just a fantasy wishing to be correct –
But it don't matter at all, as I truly despise
All Demon-rats and think the worse of them
Even when they offer me a lollipop on the
Street corner.

Oh, don't forget, Muller's henchman's cellphones wiped clean,
they ain't like me, writing it all down, then publishing it to let it
hang out there. – I meant aim.
The difference? I got a thick, long hard-on while they got small
lumps of flaccid urine emitters.

Hey, punk-head – why would a bitch want to suck your thing
when mine tastes better?

That, my friend, is Hunter's wish on a pillow.

That is, Large Capacity Magazines, still too few bullets, ten-
percent of a perfect 100,
therefore ten a failure when 100 a success.
How can I become a duplicate Eastwood
Without 100 bullets? Subway entry demands it. Going to the
local restaurant demands it. Going to the local gas station
demands it.
100 bullets the minimum –
not a 10 percent failure – for why buy ten guns when one will do
perfectly fine
equipped with the perfect magazine.
Whoever went to battle with only 10
bullets? Are you insane! 50,000 bullets the
killing average per gook in 'Nam. So, let's
be reasonable and pass in Congress a bill,
vis-à-vis Switzerland, a closet full of bullets
with 2 high powered automatics – ah, peace
at last, armed to the max. Besides, I hate
working a plowshare.

Yep, go for it, McSally and Blackburn, two sensible
Republicans, go for it, get-ta-that-money – no – that gold from
Chinaman before nukes go off in Hong Kong, no King Kong to
save them, Japan won't license him out, Taiwan awaiting, so get-
ta-money – Chinaman's a thief anyway, stealing everything he
can, so force it
out-ta his hand,
The compromise – Taiwan under its own flag, its own
sovereign country, there I said it now, and I said it a dozen time
before, Taiwan its own country, fuck China in the ass, Thatcher
set the precedent,
Standard & Poor's better get it straight,
Intellectual and manufacturing thieves need
To feel the sting of gold, not paper money – and damn be sure –
gold at 1912's value, not 2020's value – accumulative interest
not enough a factor, pay, pay, pay, chineerman, the rally call,
then to all American players in China, get out boys while ye can
still.

Sorry, I meant FUCK!
The crappers left their crap all over the
     place,
Now new shit falls everywhere from the
     mouths of delegates, Crapper-Crapper,
The Clapper wishes it was the Clapper
But no, its true, crap shit won the demon's
     Rally, already the word "President"
          (Not in error but in expectation)
Came rushing out of his mouth;
Then I saw a printed slogan,
"Joe /Hoe" and I laughed, the cameraman
Caught the picture to paste in his yearbook,
Someone knows the truth, but the speeches of the convention are
so cute and enticing, everyone forgets there are no policies,
however, who cares about policy if the slogan is catchy-dicey –
what was it?
Oh, yes,
Peace? That's it – but in the time of China and North Korea,
Biden's solution is to
Print money for bribes to henchman,
But it matters not, the crapper already shit
In his pants when, in a final moment of life,
He realized he never could be the President,
So out-of-touch with reality, his followers
Also too stupid to understand, a desolation coming up like two
hard eggs on a skillet.

Pe/lu/shit gotta get that rag on top of her head cut, no matter
what, no matter if it's violating the policy of no salons, no work,
starve to death,
no hair cut for thee, but ragged head just thinks she can get that
shit clean and curled, dyed as well, to impress her co-
conspirators on beating up Trump, her mantle dreams of
ascension to President already in place – her mind so twisted, she
forgot about how AOC created Kennedy's loss, so now her mop
atop her head needs a major overhaul above everything else in
existence to be ever so cute to clear her mind that AOC can just
slick it out like no one else can.

So fuck the world. In style I walk.

Damn, I forgot, the cameras are always on.

Now the entire world knows I'm nothing more than a haggard
old ugly rejection of a has-been, needing, like right now, this
second, a hair shampoo.

Wrong Again, Saggy Tits

Californippa a-burning again,
so saggy bitch gotta tell G7 the climate's
a-destroying us, yet so wrong stupid head, so wrongy.

It ain't climate heat,
    climate cold,
        climate rain,
            or hurricanes
or thunder bolts firing from Thor's hand.

Nope! It's a-man . . . singular . . . who is prepping
the auto destruct button,
Boon-boon-boon,
LA gone, so is New York, London,
    Shanghai, Tokyo, Moscow . . .
        gone with the boon,
not with the Furies of rain, snow and heat, but with the radio-act-
tiv-ity of us going berserky in a moment gotten away
so AOC and Demon-rats thinking you know about green earth –
you know squat shit, cause volcanoes a-going blow the ash and
cover up all the solar panels and rust all the
engines, nucky waste a-sticking to the ground and plants and
animal skins and fisheees . . . so go eat some ice cream and get
another hair cut. You don't know shit.

People don't care, they wanna revolution, so a stupid
incompetent is needed to pretend to lead the anarchist pack who
need-e a symbol, regardless that he is like the wind, tomorrow
blowing here, then there, it's a wonder his lips aren't chafed.

But wait . . . they are. So I wonder, why the fuck does a black
man who want's power wanna a white man who is powerless to
lead them? Forget all-talk half-injune girl? She's 100% for
herself. She doesn't knew know what a struggling black family
looks like.

Man-oh-ma, the Demon-rats really know how to sell shit to the
soul man who thinks it's so sweet and valuable: the white man's
burden just keeps on going while nigger
Just keeps on dropping his pants thinking his butt is all the
protest they need.

Cities burned in the 60's, but so what?
Cities burning 60 years later, but so what?
Ain't it in fact the white boys doing all the burning while blackie
just tags along? Nope, not a black movement, but a
     white movement, you hear me?
The communists are way smarter than ghetto boy who's a killing
his brothers 274 to cop's 1.

Poor Jonah, not one day of peace in the U.S.A. much less 40
days in the ancient town of Nineveh .

217,700 American fatalities!
Not one shot fired.
A Wuhan laboratory success story
Done did triumph. China smile all too
Gigantic too be ignored, yet why is it Time
Magazine writes it's an American failure? Should we retaliate
with a massive nukey-wipey-you-off-the-face-of-the-earth bomb:
Ka-boom! No more war jet superiority and no more than USA
naval ships to worry about . . . Hong Kong applause readily
given, Taiwan, finally its own country . . . but nope, Timey
writer gotta blame USA . . . doctor, doctor, where's the vaccine?
Congress, pay off New York's debt, cali's as well, then vacina-
man a-coming, no less than from Russia, no, wait, china-a-man's
got the vaccine, $6,000 a shot, who cares if it works or not:
Made in China got a reputation to cheat and lie, steal the patent,
you know. Their theft creed a culture reality, but nope, blame the
USA as a failure, and damn if America refuses to drop on its
knees sucking mongol cock.

Hey, stupid asses, your vote ain't shit to get a man elected to the Presidency. This ain't a mayor's race or city-council member's race, it's a race for the Presidency, and in that race, your vote ain't shit!!

It's the Electoral Collage that decides who is going to be the President, and your vote may – or may not – influence their final decision.

But your vote: nope, no, nada.

Stupid ass motherfucker, don't believe me? Hillary and Al Gore proved it.

In 2020, based on the census count, 538 Electors are the true power in the U.S.A. – not the millions of registered voters! Got it, dumb-ass? No? There is one Elector for each Representative in the House and one Elector for each senator.

Hey, let me make it clearer – if 51% of the state's popular vote for their favorite candidate, that candidate get 100% of the Electoral vote. That's why the USA is a REPUBLIC and not a Democracy.

Oh, hey, baby, dig this shit: the elector can vote for whomever he wants, without restriction. Oaths and fines mean nothing, shit-head! So damn, fuck. That means if 98% of the voters vote for a Demon-rat-ass the Electoral boy can still cast his vote for the Righteous Republican! Yeah, dig it!

Already happened: 7 times.

5 times Electoral College overruled the popular vote!

Twice the House of Representatives made the final decision, so voters, this is the reality of a Republic.

So why are you idiots letting that whining bitch deceive you?

Article II, Section I of the U.S. Constitution.

There. Know you know it. Rioting and burning and a-stealing the poor man's merchandise ain't getting that demon-cock elected.

*Hey Pope! Excommunicate all 12 Roman Catholics in the US
Senate*
if they refuse to
Endorse Amy Coney Barrett

Long title for a simple poem.

But the title is what it is – if ACB denied, Pope baby better get his wand moving and say "Adios" to the 12 hypocritical demon-rat members of the US Senate. Of course, this is Saturday long before the actual confirmation, but one does love to speculate, as so many CNN cronies already do.

Yet, presupposing they do vote against ACB, then it confirms they are indeed baby killers and Liberal fakers who care move about earthly power than a nice resting place in heaven. Therefore, if the 12 vote "Nay" then could it be possible that the moral souls of all 12 nonsupporting members of ACB will be eternally damned to hell, where whips and chains wait upon the arrival of their leprosy pocked bodies? I don't know. Yet, I wonder if there is enough holy water to clear them of their massive sins. I also wonder, why isn't Biden excommunicated?

Morality either wins, or it doesn't.

Fiery hell seems to be the right place to visit, perhaps eternally, because the baby killers think in demonic terms, purification impossible to attain.

Therefore, don't become like Biden who's already on hell's list. That's it. Lecture's over.

Kalank a-coming up.

Of course you knew I couldn't let this one go.
Hard drive hacked for a good cause, FBI wishing they spoke up,
but nope, favoritism always before justice. Corruption exposed,
millions gained, where's the money now? Still no arrests, Biden
better win to bury all articles forever, and damn to fuck the
reporter who says his son ain't smelling sweet every morning.

Fantasy land, turning on the TV with FBI agents placing
handcuffs on Biden and Hunter, Harris a-dancing in her living
room, ready to assume number 1 spot in a heartbeat, her grimy
smile and ugly eyes facing the camera with a fuck you all smirk.

Feinstein's hug a pleasant enactment amidst contention, a nice gesture I thought, but goddamn it, the far-left now hate your guts and want you expulsed to hell, kicked out and roasted on a bundle of pine needles.

Since you're old and worn out, and obvious out of your mind, vote for Amy because the aim is straight at you by your liberal ass citizens of cali-dally-mally.

Convert to a Republican and go down in the history books as the greatest stateswoman Cali ever had.

Mmmmmmmm!